Before this morning, Pig's nose had never squeaked – not even once.

Squeak!

But since this morning, all it ever did was squeak.

It squeaked during breakfast.

It squeaked while
he was feeding
pigeons in the park.

Squeak!

And it squeaked
non-stop in the bath.

Pig
AND
small

by Alex Latimer

PICTURE CORGI

for Sophie, Lily & Olivia

PIG AND SMALL
A PICTURE CORGI BOOK
978 0 552 56543 1
Published in Great Britain

by Picture Corgi, an imprint of Random House
Children's Publishers UK A Random House Group Company
This edition published 2 0 1 3
1 3 5 7 9 10 8 6 4 2
Copyright © Alex Latimer, 2013

Picture Corgi Books are
published by Random House
Children's Publishers UK, 61-63
Uxbridge Road, London W5 5SA

www.randomhouse
childrens.co.uk
www.randomhouse.co.uk
Addresses for companies
within The Random House Group
Limited can be found at:
www.randomhouse.co.uk/
offices.htm THE RANDOM
HOUSE GROUP Limited Reg.
No954009 A CIP catalogue
record for this book
is available from
the British Library.
Printed in China

MIX
Paper from
responsible sources
FSC® C104723

The Random House Group Limited supports The Forest Stewardship Council®(FSC®), the leading international
forest-certification organisation. Our books carrying the FSC label are printed on FSC®-certified paper. FSC is the
only forest-certification scheme supported by the leading environmental organisations, including Greenpeace.
Our paper procurement policy can be found at www.randomhouse.co.uk/environment

So Pig got the big medical book down from his bookshelf, and looked up Squeaky Nose Syndrome.

Squeaky Jaw Syndrome
Squeaky Knee Syndrome
Squeaky Leg Syndrome
eaky Mouth Syndrome
ky Oesophagus Syndrome
Squeaky Pants Syndrome

But there was nothing in the book about it.

Pig touched his nose
– it felt normal.

Then he breathed in
through his nostrils.
They worked fine.

Finally he squinted
and peered down
his snout.

And there, standing on the end of his nose, was a tiny bug, and it was waving and squeaking like mad!

"Hello," said Pig.
"Squeak, squeak," replied Bug.

Pig could tell by the way the bug was waving and squeaking that it wanted to be friends.

So Pig got his tandem
bicycle out of the shed . . .

and Pig and Bug rode down
to the park together.

But Pig couldn't help feeling as though he'd done most of the pedalling.

To make up for Pig having to do all the work, Bug gave Pig a delicious cake he'd baked that very morning.

But Pig just ate the whole thing in one go without appreciating the way Bug had decorated it.

"How about a game of chess to cheer you up?" asked Pig.

But by the time Bug had
made the first move . . .

Pig was fast asleep.

When Pig woke up, Bug had knitted a matching pair of jumpers – one for himself and one for Pig.

But although Pig said he liked his new jumper
very much, he couldn't fit it over his head.

Pig and Bug were very sad. They'd tried so hard to be friends, but it just wasn't working.

So they said goodbye . . .

and parted ways.

But just then, as Pig
was walking away,
the wind picked up
and blew a newspaper
right into his face.

And this is what Pig saw:

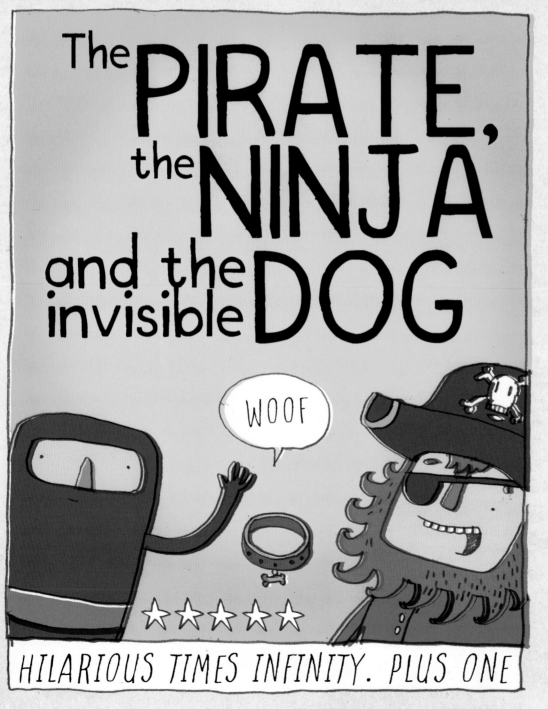

MOVIES TODAY

The **PIRATE,** the **NINJA** and the invisible **DOG**

WOOF

★★★★★

HILARIOUS TIMES INFINITY. PLUS ONE

THE PIRATE, THE NINJA AND THE INVISIBLE DOG

A pirate runs aground on deserted island, only to fin it inhabited by a pack o ferocious invisible dogs. H befriends one and the escape together on a raft They are adrift at sea fo months when all of sudden, a time-travellin ninja appears on their raf and begins karate choppin the logs on which they'r sitting. After persuadin him to stop, the pirat takes his two new friend on an adventure in the hig seas where they meet a sa squid, a cowardly cowboy a troupe of sea monkey and an astronaut who ha lost his helmet. This is fantastic movie for all age and will no doubt be classic to be watched an re-watched for years t come.

*****

Squeak?

Pig rushed off
to the cinema.

"A ticket for one seat please – my
friend will sit on my ear. And just
one box of popcorn," said Pig.

"Bug doesn't eat much at all."

POPCORN

They were almost late for the start of the show, but Bug helped Pig to find the way to their seat in record time.

Then the film started.

When Bug got scared, he hid behind Pig's ear.

Aha hah hah ha

And when Pig didn't get a joke, Bug explained it to him.

When the film was finished, they walked home and talked all about it.

They were thrilled they'd found something that they both enjoyed doing. It made them think of a few other things they could do together as friends.

The next day they
visited an art gallery,

and the aquarium

and the theatre.

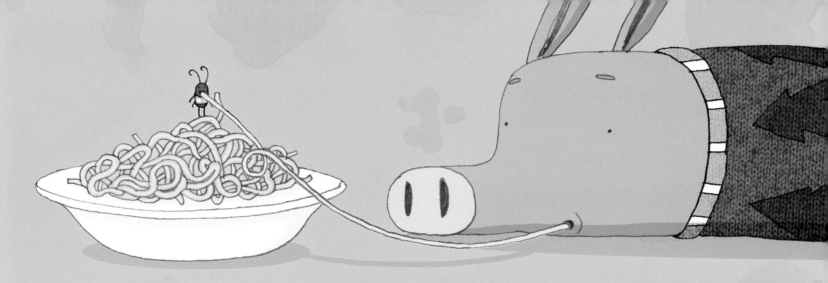

They ate out at a restaurant,

spent a few hours at the zoo

and relaxed on the beach.

They had a great time,
and they found that they
had loads in common.

Of course there were still things that they didn't enjoy doing together.

Bug didn't like playing catch.

And Pig didn't like playing hide and seek.

Bug always found him in a flash . . .

but finding Bug took days.

But there were lots more things
that they did enjoy doing together.

They forgot that one of them was big and the other was small – best friends don't care about silly things like that.